# There Goes Lowell's Party!

by Esther Hershenhorn

illustrated by Jacqueline Rogers

*Holiday House / New York*

In the whole of Crumm County, past Piggott's Peak and Slocum's Bluff, no one loved his birthday better than Lowell.

No siree.

From one spring to the next, past summer, fall, and winter, Lowell rose each morning saying, "Hey, there, sun!" Next he'd X out the date on his trusty calendar, peeking at the pages, gauging the months and weeks to go.

On the long-awaited day, it was the sun who found Lowell hugging himself on his front porch step.

"It's my birthday, Lucky!" Lowell told his hound.

"And my party, Queenie!" Lowell told his cat.

The sky drew a sigh. Lowell hurried for the door.

Lowell found his Mama fixing cupcakes in the kitchen.

"The sun sent me a present, Mama!" Lowell declared. "The morning sky, as red as your prize roses."

"Mercy, Lowell!" Mama stopped and kissed him. "Don't you know, Lovey? Red skies mean rain."

"Yep," piped 'retta Sue, "so there goes your party. Spring rains these parts are cat and dog pourdowns."

"Yep," piped Earl. "Mama, hold those cupcakes. Crumm Creek will flood. Not one Crumm will come."

Lowell checked the family pictures hanging in the parlor.
Soon he set to lining tins, filling them with batter.
"I know Mama's side can log-ride here."

Lowell tied rag bows to his porch and picket fence.
"There'll be cousins right and left, Lucky, one o'clock sharp."
Geese flocked low while the sun played hide-and-seek.
Lowell cupped his ear. Twice. Then he hurried home.

Lowell found his Papa fixing ice cream on the porch.

"Geese honked and hello-ed, Papa!" Lowell declared. " 'Happy Birthday, Lowell!' on account of today."

"Shucks and shoot, Lowell!" Papa stopped and held him. "Don't you know, Sonny? Low geese mean rain."

"Yep," crooned 'retta Sue, "so there goes your party. Pourdowns mean waves of mud. Hollows wash up whole."

"Yep," crooned Earl. "Papa, hold that ice cream. Piggott's Peak is history. Not a Piggott will come."

Lowell checked the family pictures hanging in the parlor.

Soon he set to brimming Papa's ice tub with cream.

"I know Papa's side can keg-slide here."

Lowell tied balloons to the mailbox by the road.
"There'll be cousins to the rafters, Queenie, party games and more."
Dust puffs rose, swirling north with bits and twigs.
Something tickled Lowell's cheek. Lowell hurried home.

Lowell found his Granny fixing lemonade out back.

"Our oak grove waved, Granny!" Lowell declared. "Three times and then some, since it's my day."

"Sakes alive, Lowell!" Granny stopped and hugged him. "Don't you know, Sweetum? Leaf backs mean rain."

"Yep," tuned 'retta Sue, "so there goes your party. Pourdowns mean twirling gales. Towns get blown and thrown."

"Yep," tuned Earl. "Granny, hold that lemonade. Slocum's Bluff's a goner. Your Slocum folk won't come."

Lowell checked the family pictures hanging in the parlor.

Soon he set to juicing lemons, topping Granny's crock.

"Granny's side can fly on vines. I know that for sure."

Lowell posted party signs, then sat beside the creek.

"Have you ever seen black clouds, Lucky, prettier than those? Sheep, that's what they look like, all woolly and close."

"And listen, Queenie, to those mockingbirds singing. Loud and long. That's the 'Happy Birthday Song.'"

Lowell eyed his kin grabbing wash from the line.

Raindrops pelted Lowell's turned-up palms.

"Told you!" sang 'retta Sue.

"Told you so!" sang Earl.

Lowell tramped home, mumbling, "Told you so yourselves!"

Lowell set out birthday treats, then party-fixed the parlor.
Rain *thrumped* the roof. Mama's pictures swung and swayed.
Winds rattled doors and panes. Papa's pictures wobbled.
Thunderclaps dropped Granny's pictures crashing to the floor.
"Know what, Lucky?"
Lowell sensed trouble.
"Know what, Queenie? Maybe they're not coming. 'retta Sue and Earl
were right. There goes my party . . . . . . . . . . . . ."

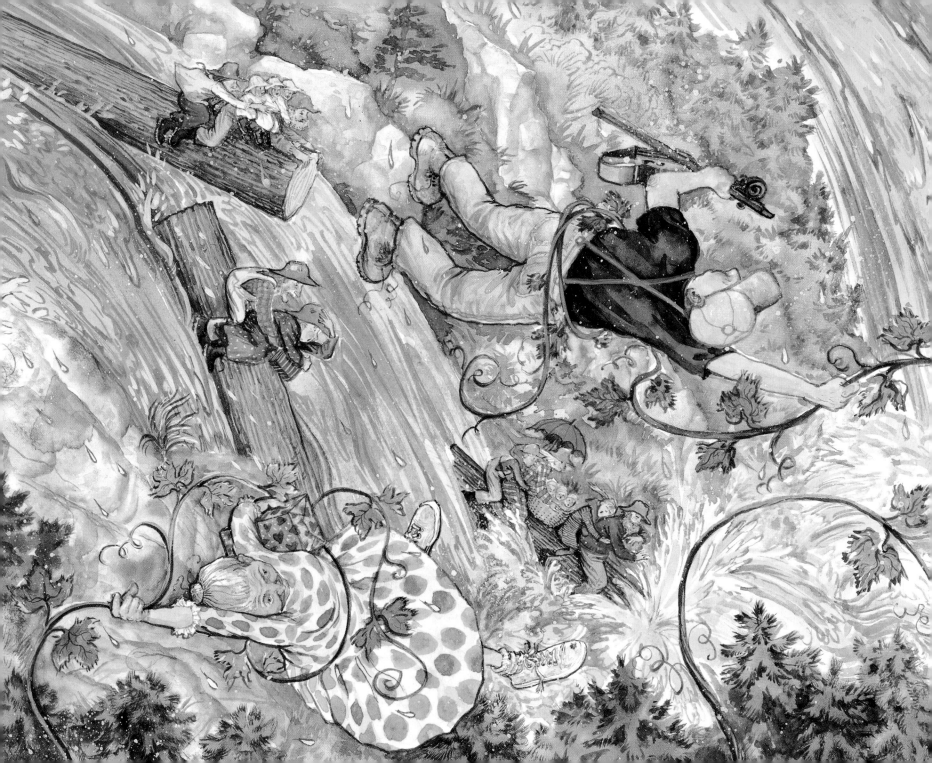

"**YOO-HOO's**!" beckoned.
Lowell checked the view.
"My gosh! A birthday ark! I knew it!"
Lowell flew.

Lowell found his family in the front hall fixing leaks.

"HERE COMES MY BIRTHDAY PARTY!" Lowell declared. "Two by two, under bumbershoots and booted."

"Now we know!" Lowell's folks and Granny hooted. "Rain means nothing when it comes to one like you!"

Lowell elbowed 'retta Sue. "Yep," she agreed.

Lowell elbowed Earl. "Yep," he agreed too.

Howls and meows and "Hey's!" made quite a din, once Lowell led his kin, "All together, 'Come on in!'"

The sun let the moon chase Lowell's party guests home. Five good-night kisses chased Lowell off to bed.

"The moon made me a birthday present!" Lowell declared. "A big fat ring with five fat stars."

Lowell's kin chorused, "Happy Birthday, Lowell!"

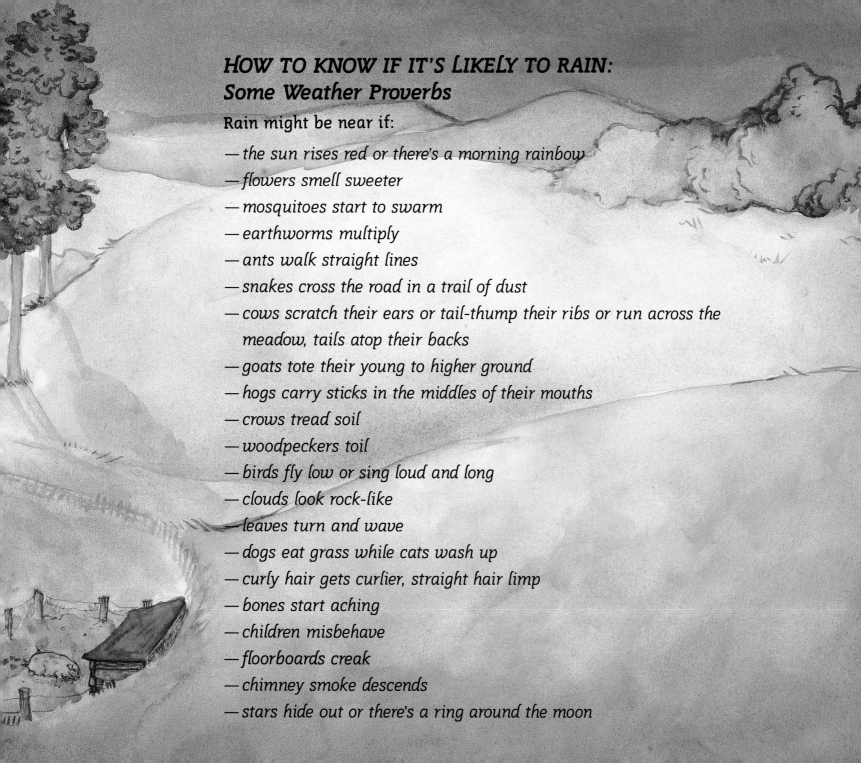

## HOW TO KNOW IF IT'S LIKELY TO RAIN:
### Some Weather Proverbs

Rain might be near if:

— the sun rises red or there's a morning rainbow

— flowers smell sweeter

— mosquitoes start to swarm

— earthworms multiply

— ants walk straight lines

— snakes cross the road in a trail of dust

— cows scratch their ears or tail-thump their ribs or run across the
   meadow, tails atop their backs

— goats tote their young to higher ground

— hogs carry sticks in the middles of their mouths

— crows tread soil

— woodpeckers toil

— birds fly low or sing loud and long

— clouds look rock-like

— leaves turn and wave

— dogs eat grass while cats wash up

— curly hair gets curlier, straight hair limp

— bones start aching

— children misbehave

— floorboards creak

— chimney smoke descends

— stars hide out or there's a ring around the moon

To Jon, of course:
May you always march forth

Love,
E.H.


To the memory of Zach Culley.

J.R.


Special thanks to Libby Lancaster, Darryl and Judy Roberts, Jean and Randi at B. & B.,
and my children, Martha and Emma, and Esther.

J.R.

*Text copyright © 1998 by Esther Hershenhorn*
*Illustrations copyright © 1998 by Jacqueline Rogers*
ALL RIGHTS RESERVED
*Printed in the United States of America*
FIRST EDITION
Library of Congress Cataloging-in-Publication Data
Hershenhorn, Esther.
There goes Lowell's party! / by Esther Hershenhorn; illustrated
by Jacqueline Rogers.
p.    cm.
Summary: Lowell refuses to believe that a brewing storm will keep
his resourceful Ozark relatives from celebrating his birthday.
Includes a list of rain-related proverbs.
ISBN 0-8234-1313-6
[1. Rain and rainfall — Fiction.    2. Storms — Fiction.
3. Birthdays — Fiction.    4. Ozark Mountains — Fiction.]    I. Rogers,
Jacqueline, ill.    II. Title.
PZ7.H432425Th        1998        96-40168        CIP        AC
[E] — dc21